Our Little Polish Cousin

Florence E. Mendel

Our Little Polish Cousin

CHAPTER I

THE ORIGIN OF POLAND

WE cross the Atlantic Ocean in one of the great floating palaces which sail from New York; after seven days of good times on board, with not too much sea-sickness, we sight land, the glorious, sunny land of France. We all know and love France, for it has been endeared to us in many ways. Lafayette helped us in our time of need long years ago, and the French school-children have given us that token of their esteem, the Goddess of Liberty, which stands at the entrance of the harbor in New York, a welcome to all the poor, homeless refugees and immigrants who come to this beloved land of ours in search of rest.

After passing through the custom-house at Havre, and our baggage being examined by the officials in charge, to see that we have brought nothing dutiable into their country, we board the waiting train, and are whirled along by the side of the sparkling river Seine, which winds its way lazily among beautiful green fields under the highest state of cultivation, mostly in vegetables, until we reach the charming city of Paris. As we may not linger here, much as we should love to, we are off again in the morning. We leave behind us the sunny, fair skies of France and emerge into the peaceful country of Germany with its rows upon rows of hops so symmetrically strung upon high poles, and its fertile vegetable gardens, where we see whole families, from the old grandparents, much too old to labor, down to the tiny but sturdy four-year-old, bending over the growing plants, weeding and hoeing and ridding of plant-pests. To see the endless truck gardens, as we pass by in the Schnell-zug (express train), one would be justified in believing that the people of Europe ate nothing but vegetables. And it is quite true. The masses have little else to feed upon, as meat is a rarity in poor families. Even the salaried people are not able to afford that luxury more than once a week, and then it frequently happens that only the head of the house may indulge.

As night descends, our train pulls in at the depot at Dresden; but this is not Poland; a little further, and we find ourselves in the city of Cracow, the ancient city of Chief Krakus, which we find nestled snugly and boldly at the junction of the three powerful countries, Russia, Austria-Hungary and Germany. It is here we purpose spending a cycle of months visiting, as Cracow is most typically Polish, with its surrounding vicinities.

What a glorious country we are in! It is true, it is broad, and flat and low, with rugged mountains and rapid rivers separating it, one part from another; nevertheless, it is a wonderful land. At one time it was a large country: now it is divided into three parts, each belonging to a different nation, the Russians, the Austrians and the Germans. The conquering nations have tried very hard to introduce their own customs into this captive land, but the Polacks will not accept them. We shall not enter into this phase of the question, but will visit the native as he is and not as the conquerors would have him.

It is very much more interesting to know just where the country lies about which we are reading, so we shall first learn where Poland lies upon the map of Europe. We open our books, and search the map through, but there is no country marked Poland. We are grieved to say there is no longer any country by that name; it was not enough to wrest the country asunder, but even its very name must be torn from it; therefore, it is in the southwestern part of Russia, the very northeast tip of Austria-Hungary, and the ragged northeast portion of Germany that we must trace the boundaries of Poland. From Riga on the north to the Black Sea on the south Poland had ample outlets for its great quantities of wheat and sugar which it raised, and which brought enormous wealth into the country.

Everything must have a beginning, even countries, and Poland was no exception. It wasn't like Topsy, who wasn't ever born but just "growed;" so here is the story of the birth of Poland.

Once upon a time, oh, very long ago, there lived a king or chief over the lands which lay near the mouth of the Danube River. Now you all know that the Danube rises at the Black Sea on the west, quite close to the southern border of Russia. This chief had three sons, who were great, strong men. At length the king died, leaving his lands and all his wealth to the care of these sons. Now, in those far-away days, the tribes who lived thereabouts were very savage; they had no learning or education. All they cared for was to fight, and make conquests of other nations so as to enlarge their own possessions. When the three brothers found themselves left with their father's small domain, they were not satisfied. They could not all rule upon the same throne and be at peace, one with the other. The estate was too small to divide into three separate kingdoms. Consequently, they determined to go in search of other lands which would be large enough to satisfy their demands. They set out and journeyed along happily for some time, meeting with many dangers by the way, for the land was full of wild beasts of all sorts, dangerous reptiles and savage men, who were worse, indeed, than all the wild things of the earth.

While walking along the highroad, one of the brothers chanced to gaze upward. He saw three eagles high in the air. He thought nothing of this, however, for the air was full of all sorts of birds, large and small. But finally he noticed that the birds were following along with them. At last the brothers began to joke about the incident.

"I choose the white bird," said Lekh, the eldest.

"And I the black one," said Russ.

"Then I must take the only one left," remarked Tchekh. And, in this merry manner, they passed the time as they continued their march.

At length the travellers came to three roads, diverging like the rays of a fan. One road led to the north, the direction they were then pursuing; another turned to the northeast, and the third to the northwest.

"Which shall we take?" asked one of them, as they halted their footsteps in order to decide the important question.

"I am for going straight on," Lekh said.

"And I, too," spoke up the other. "There is no use in separating so soon. Let us wait a while!"

As they were arguing the point back and forth, Lekh saw the white eagle, his eagle, winging its way due north. The other two birds were each following the direction of the other two diverging roads.

"There goes your bird," Lekh said to his brother Russ, as he pointed to the black eagle flying toward the right. "Mine goes straight onward, and so shall I. As for the rest of you, you may do what you like."

"Then I shall follow my bird," Russ replied. "Perhaps it will bring us good luck."

So the three brothers bade one another an affectionate farewell and parted. Russ followed the black eagle until he came to the present country of Russia, which he founded and named. Tchekh founded the country of Bohemia, the people of which are even to-day known as Czechs; as for Lekh, he wandered due north until he came to the broad plain where he settled. As his guide had been a white eagle, he thought it but appropriate to make that his emblem; and, in this way, it happened that Poland has a white eagle upon its flag.

Lekh, as I have just said, settled in an immense plain, the Polish word for which is "Pola." Then Lekh added his own name to that, making Po-Lekh, sometimes written Lakh, and now we have the word Po-lakh, meaning the people of Lekh who lived in the plain.

CHAPTER II

THE ARRIVAL AT THE DWÓR

IT was snowing fast. The flakes fell in great, thick showers about the occupants of the heavy sleigh, who were fairly covered in a blanket of white, crisp snow. The driver lashed his sturdy, thoroughbred beasts with his long-handled whip, for they were in danger of becoming hopelessly sunk in the heavy drifts which filled the road, and there were yet some miles to go. The sleigh-bells jingled merrily, nevertheless. What cared they whether they were snow-bound or not, so long as they could make their music ring out over the clear, frosty air? It was their purpose in life to chime, and they were doing their best. The harder the horses tugged and the more they floundered about in the great drifts, the more merrily the bells rang out. Some one must keep good-natured, and so they took that task upon themselves. Happy bells!

The horses panted and halted a moment for the much-needed rest. The driver slapped his great arms across his chest to keep the circulation moving; but the occupants in the rear of the sleigh made no motion whatever. For all one could see of them, the sleigh might have been empty except as to fur robes, for not even the tip of a nose was visible. As the driver called out to his team, "Gee up," one corner of the fur robe in the rear seat moved, and a little voice piped up:

"Mother, are we almost there?"

"Just a little while yet, my dear," the mother replied, as she raised her head from the protecting warmth of the robe and looked about her. "I can see the tall trees of the drive now, just ahead of us. Peep your head out, Jan, and see if you can catch sight of grandfather's dwór," said Mrs. Teczynska, as she rearranged the robes so that Jan could sit upright.

Before them, some mile away, lay an immense park enclosed within a high stone fence. The sleigh made headway easier now, for the road about the entrance to the dwór was in better condition than the ordinary public road. Soon they passed the stone brama or gateway, sped down the splendid broad driveway lined on both sides with overhanging trees, mounted the rise at the top, and with a whoop and a hurrah, the driver pulled rein at the porch of the dwór or country-home of Mr. Ostrowski, the father of Mrs. Teczynska.

The tinkle of the sleigh bells had announced the arrival of the guests long before they had reached the porch; and the entire family, big and little, with innumerable servants, were awaiting within the reception-hall to greet the newcomers.

The villa was just the hospitable-looking home in which to meet at the Christmas season. One knew, from its very appearance, that it sheltered a warm welcome. It was built of stone, was two stories high and had a red-tiled roof; red chimneys dotted it all over; you never did see so many chimneys all on one house before. There was an immense veranda running along the entire front of the house, supported by heavy columns, giving it a most substantial air, the air of a home and not merely an expensive residence.

Mr. Ostrowski assisted his daughter and the little grandson Jan to disentangle themselves from the heavy fur robes, and they were hurried into the warm reception-room, where a bright fire was burning on an open hearth. As Mrs. Teczynska passed through the massive front door, which was opened for her by an elderly, not to say old, man-servant, she greeted him kindly.

"And how does Henryk find himself?"

"HENRYK LEANED DOWN AND KISSED THE HAND OF THE LITTLE FELLOW"

The old man, toothless and very infirm, bowed respectfully.

"Thank you, Mlle. Martha, I keep very well; but it does my old eyes good to see you once more. How you have grown!"

"This is the little Jan, Henryk," Mrs. Teczynska said, as she drew her little son toward the old man. Henryk leaned down and kissed the hand of the little fellow, and tears dimmed his eyes. He had been an old and trusted servant of the family for many, many years, long before Mrs. Teczynska had been born, and was now relegated to the position of doorkeeper, being much too infirm for other duties. Although it is not necessary to have a man sitting in attendance at the front door, yet it is the Polish custom in the upper circles, so as to give employment to as many peasants as possible, and for this service, they receive but a pittance, yet it suffices. It makes the aged feel independent, and that they are not a burden in the already overburdened family.

What a happy reunion! Such hugging and bustle! All the children of the Ostrowski family were once more gathered together under the home-roof for the Christmas season, which was now at the beginning.

Mr. Ostrowski, the father, was a tall man of spare build; he had the kind, blue eye of the Slav and his heavy head of brown hair was tinged slightly with white. He wore a long coat, quite resembling a dressing-gown, edged with fur about the bottom and along the front, and tied about his waist with a long sash of crimson silk. This was the house costume of Mr. Ostrowski, who leaned toward the former luxurious style of dress in Poland.

His wife was a handsome woman, even in her elderly years; her complexion was as fresh and rosy as a young matron's, and her eye as soft a blue as in her younger days. The Polish women of culture do not age; they live a life of luxury and ease, and Time is gentle with them. But for all their seeming idleness they devote many hours of each day among their poor, and Mrs. Ostrowska was no exception to this rule.

Besides the father and mother, there was the younger brother, Peter, a tall, manly-looking fellow of about sixteen years, and Marya, the young sister, who had just passed her fourteenth birthday. Then there was the married sister, Mrs. Lechowicz, her husband and two sons, Francis and Frederic, and the oldest brother, Jan Ostrowski, with his wife and two children, Ignace and Marcella. You may well believe there was much to tell each other, and a great deal of commotion, for the married children lived in dwórs of their own or in the city, and were separated, not only by distance, but by family cares and business interests, so that it was not more often than at the Christmas season they were able to meet.

Jan Teczynski was overwhelmed with so many cousins and aunts and uncles; he was but five years old, and had not made their acquaintance before. He gazed about him in wonderment at all he saw; he could not withdraw his big, blue eyes from the immense boar's head which decorated the chimney-piece, and he asked all sorts of questions concerning it. It amused the older children immensely to hear him ask who had killed it. When told his grandfather had done so, he was very proud to think that his grandfather had been so brave; then he wanted to know if the boar had hurt grandfather with his sharp, curved tusks; but Mr. Ostrowski laughingly told him he had not been harmed, whereupon Jan seemed much relieved. But when he inquired if grandfather was sure the boar had been quite dead before he had cut off its head, the other children burst into roars of merriment. Jan didn't think it a matter to laugh over at all, but from that day he regarded his grandfather as one of the bravest men in the whole world.

The young folks now made off for sports of their own, while Mrs. Teczynska, much fatigued after her long and tiresome journey, went at once to her room to rest before luncheon should be served.

The maid-servant carried up the valises and bags of Mrs. Teczynska and set them down in the room that she had occupied from childhood. Fresh, hot water being brought by yet another maid, and cool drinking water placed upon the night-stand by the side of the great bed, the servants retired and left Mrs. Teczynska alone in her old, familiar room.

It was a very large room, as are all the rooms in Polish homes. The floor was beautifully inlaid in a fancy design with hardwoods of two colors, and polished so highly one had to walk carefully so as not to fall. Against one wall stood a magnificent stove of white glazed tile, with a door of shining brass, most exquisitely designed, and which could be closed so tightly that not one bit of dust or ash could penetrate through into the room. The peculiarity of this stove was, that only half of it was in the room; the other half extended into the adjoining room, so that, in this manner, one stove did duty for two rooms, thus saving expense, space and chimneys. It reached, too, quite to the ceiling; but, as the ceiling was low, it was not as tall as many other European stoves.

And the bed! It looked quite like any other wooden bed, but what a covering! There were no sheets or blankets such as we have. Instead, there was a blue silk comforter of down, so light you would have thought there was nothing in it, daintily tied here and there with little strands of silk. This silk comforter was put over a white linen sheet, much larger every way than the comforter; the edges were then folded over the silk and buttoned to it, the button-holes being worked in the border of the sheet and the buttons placed upon the comforter. At the top, which we usually turn over the blanket, the sheet was shaped like a triangle. In the middle of the point was worked the monogram of the hostess, while the remainder of the space was filled with the most elaborate and exquisite embroidery imaginable, done by the young peasant girls upon the estate. This was not a "company" sheet; no, indeed, not at all; the same kind was used every day in the week and in the year. The pillows, too, were covered with blue silk, and over this was buttoned, just to fit, a handsome pillow-case all inset with lace insertion so that the color of the silk beneath might show through. What a luxurious bed in which to sleep! It certainly was inviting.

In one corner of the room stood a small altar to the Holy Virgin, upon which stood freshly gathered flowers from the greenhouses of the estate, and wax candles were burning. As the majority of the Polacks are Roman Catholics, these altars are found in almost every home, each bedroom having its own altar for its occupant's special devotion.

Four large windows, opening inwards like double doors, looked over the covered veranda without, toward the fields stretching as far as the eye could see, covered now with their blanket of snow, while further yet lay great forests, the tops of whose trees were barely discernible in the dim distance.

Just below the windows lay a most magnificent garden, with fountains and bordered walks; but they, too, like everything else, lay under their blanket of winter's white. The ponds beyond, which supplied the estate with fresh fish, were frozen solid, and here the children had gone for an hour's skating in the crisp air, while their childish voices carried up to where Mrs. Teczynska lay resting upon her couch.

CHAPTER III

THE SENDING OF THE OPLATKI

AT the luncheon table there was great excitement. Something was astir in the air.

"Take your time, children," Mr. Ostrowski said forcibly, as he watched their hurried anxiety. "Brother Paul will be here shortly; but there is p-l-e-n-t-y of time."

"We wish he had come before luncheon," spoke up Peter. "It is now almost too late for Cousin Frederic to receive his oplatki before Christmas."

"A few hours more or less, my son," Mrs. Ostrowska answered, "will make very little difference. We could not have Brother Paul come sooner because we were waiting for your sister to arrive. We all wanted to be together to receive the good Brother."

Turning toward her eldest daughter, Mrs. Lechowicz, she continued:

"Brother Paul, as well as the priest, has had his hands full this winter. There has been a great deal of sickness among the poor."

"It has been so in our part of the country, too," replied the daughter. "It seems to be a bad year all round."

"The crops are poor; but we are thankful to say there will be sufficient for our own people. What the rest of Poland's poor will do, it is difficult to say. I had planned to take the children to Cracow for St. John's Night—"

"Oh, mother," interrupted the young Marya, "will you?"

"Don't interrupt, Marya; it is very bad manners. I was going to say," Mrs. Ostrowska continued, addressing her children, "I had planned to take you to the feast of St. John's Night in the City if all went well upon the estate. But I know you would not care to go and enjoy yourselves if there were sickness and distress here at home among our people."

"But June is so far away," the young girl pleaded, "there is yet lots of time for a good season."

"But illness lingers," the mother added.

"I will join you, mother," Mrs. Teczynska spoke up. "It will not be a long run up and Jan would love to see the celebration of the Wianki, I am sure."

"Let us all plan to go," added the younger married daughter. "It would be great fun."

"And will you take us?" added a chorus of young voices from around the great table, while expectant faces beamed.

"Yes, all of you," the elders replied in one voice.

"What is it all about, mother?" Jan managed to say, after vainly endeavoring for some time to edge in his question.

"Once every year," Mrs. Teczynska replied, "in the city of Cracow, where we got off the train and took the sleigh to come up here, the people have a holiday. They call it the celebration of the Wianki, or wreaths, and it takes place on the twenty-fourth day of June, which is the eve of St. John's Night. They have fireworks and all sorts of gayeties."

"But what does it all mean?" the child persisted.

"Well," his mother continued, seeing that the child did not comprehend as the older children did, "many, many years ago there was a good and very wise king in Cracow named Krakus. He had a most beautiful daughter, Wanda, who was so handsome that the fame of her beauty travelled all over the country. Princes and noblemen from other lands sent their messengers to ask her hand in marriage; but the Princess Wanda did not care for any of them. At length, a fierce, determined German prince, named Rytyger, fell so madly in love with the princess that he swore he would win her for his own. But the father of the princess had meantime died, leaving her in full possession of the kingdom; and, whether it was really the fair princess Rytyger craved, or the kingdom over which she ruled, we may not know for a certainty. However that may be, he sent his messengers to ask her hand in marriage, but the Princess Wanda promptly refused his offer. As soon as the envoys returned with the refusal, Prince Rytyger was more determined than ever to possess the Polish princess. He wrote her a most impertinent letter, demanding that she become his wife at once or else he would march into her domains and carry her off, whether she were willing or not. The Princess Wanda read the letter from the haughty German prince. She set her lips hard with firm determination. If he were determined, so was she. Without a moment's loss of time, she gathered her army together, marched out of Poland and into the country of the German prince. She sent word to him of her arrival, and added that she meant to give battle. The prince was very much surprised at this news, you may be certain; however, there was nothing to do but accept the challenge so long as he had been the one to open the argument. After the battle was finished many of the Germans were left upon the field, while Wanda returned to her castle-fortress of Wawel in Cracow.

"Seeing there was no use to refuse the offers of marriage that were made her, and fearing that other foreign princes might come into her land and wage war against her subjects on her account, she jumped from the top of the great stone wall that surrounded her palace, and fell into the river Vistula, which runs at the foot. And ever since, the Polish people have commemorated her death by casting wreaths into the river, at about the spot where Princess Wanda jumped into the waters. This is the meaning of the feast of St. John's Eve celebration of the Wianki."

"I should love to see it," the little fellow said, after a few moments' silence. "Will you surely take me?"

"Yes, indeed, if the other little cousins go," his mother replied. "When I was a little girl, like your Aunt Marya here," she continued, glancing at her young sister, "I went to the celebration. And you will open your eyes wide, Jan, I'll tell you that."

"Oh, goody, I wish it was the twenty-fourth of June now."

"But we have the Christmas season now," his grandfather spoke up. "That is much better, for we are all together. We have the fine snow for sleighing and snowballing. We have the ponds to skate upon, and we have—the Jaselki."

"What's that?" little Jan asked.

"Jan, dear," his mother said, "please do not ask so many questions. Let your grandfather finish before you interrupt."

"But he says so many things I don't know anything about," the child answered.

"That is right, Martha," Mr. Ostrowski said, "let the little chap learn. Of course he doesn't know what the Jaselki are, for he is too little to know everything. But that is a secret, Jan," the grandfather continued, as he shook a gentle finger at the boy. "You will see something wonderful at this Christmas season."

The maid entered; she said a few words in a low tone to Mrs. Ostrowska, and left the room.

"How we have lingered!" the grandmother said, as she rose from her seat at the table. "Brother Paul has been waiting some little time. Let us all rise to greet him!"

As they obeyed, the door at the farther end of the long dining-room opened, and a monk, clad in a long black robe with a girdle of rope about his waist, stood upon the threshold. In his hand he held his black beaver hat, and under his arm was a small package upon which the children kept their eyes assiduously glued.

"Welcome, Brother Paul," Mr. Ostrowski said as he greeted the monk. "The little folks have been in a fever of impatience; you are well come."

"I hear the same story in every home," the monk replied, as he turned and smiled at the row of happy faces. "They are all anxious for their oplatki."

"Let us go into the library," Mr. Ostrowski said, as he threw open the heavy doors communicating with that room; "the fire burns brightly there, and you must be cold."

"It certainly is raw without," the monk replied. "We are to have a long, hard winter, I fear."

"We just arrived this morning, Brother Paul," Mrs. Teczynska said. "We had a dreadfully cold ride from Cracow. I thought little Jan's nose would be nipped."

"Come here, son, and let's see if Jack Frost got away with any of it," the monk said.

The little fellow obeyed with a very serious face. He had quite an awe for the brotherhood; he held up his face for inspection.

"I believe it's all there," the brother laughingly said, as he examined the boy's serious face. "But you had a narrow escape."

Brother Paul drew up to the great table in the centre of the room, having sufficiently warmed his numbed hands at the welcome fire. Surrounded by the anxious, waiting children he untied the package he had brought. With keen interest they watched the monk draw forth a neat packet which he handed to Mr. Ostrowski, who untied it. Within, lay a quantity of small, round wafers, thin enough to be almost transparent, made from flour and water, upon each of which was impressed a religious picture. Upon one was the image of the Christ, another bore the resemblance of the manger, or of a saint.

"I shall get mine off right away," Peter said. "May I?" turning to his father.

Seeing there was no holding back the children's impetuosity, Mrs. Ostrowska handed the children some of the oplatki, which they at once proceeded to enclose in letters already waiting.

"I hope Cousin Frederic will get this before Christmas Day," Peter said, "but it is pretty late."

The rest of the afternoon was spent in writing letters and sending off the oplatki or Christmas cards to such of the relatives as were unable to be present with the family at this season. It is as much an event in Polish families to send these cards as it is with us; they bear messages of love and good-will, although they have no verses upon them. The priest of the village has put his blessing upon them, and these blessings go forth to the dear, absent ones. No written sentiment is necessary, for the absent know that the home-folks are thinking of them. It is a beautiful custom, and if it should happen that any of you children should receive an oplatki at the Christmas season, you will know what it is meant to convey.

Perhaps some of you more observant readers have remarked the difference in spelling the name of Mr. Ostrowski and his wife. While Mr. Ostrowski's name ends in "i," his wife's name ends with an "a;" this is simply a peculiarity of the Polish language, being the masculine and feminine ending of the name.

CHAPTER IV

CHRISTMAS AT THE DWÓR

MR. TECZYNSKI arrived the day before Christmas; business had detained him until then. Jan was delighted to see his father again, from whom he had never been separated so long. Three weeks seemed a very long time to him. He had had such a glorious time at grandfather's, though, with the new cousins and the uncles and the aunts, he had quite forgotten everybody and everything, except when bedtime came. Then he missed his father greatly, for there was no one to tell him his customary stories, and Papa Teczynski was a famous story-teller.

There was no one at home to receive Mr. Teczynski, except little Jan; the entire family had gone to the village to attend service. But then, Jan's father did not mind that; he was glad to be alone with his little son for a while; they had so many things to tell each other, and the time passed too rapidly. They did not even notice that the hour was getting late and that the electric lamps were lighted, nor did they hear the return of the others from their devotions. There is no festival in the land of Poland which is observed with as much rigor and ceremony as that of the Christmas season. Almost the entire day is spent in fasting and prayer, after which comes the evening meal.

Scarcely were the family returned, and the greetings over between them and the new arrival, than dinner was announced. With great ceremony, they formed in line, the father and mother leading the way, and in this most formal manner the family procession passed through the high folding doors opening from the library into the immense dining-hall. There were few occasions during the year when the younger children were allowed the privilege of sitting at the dinner table with their parents; and these occasions were most awe-inspiring to them. But upon this Christmas Eve there was an atmosphere of reserve and restraint in the attitude of the elders which had its quieting effect upon the younger ones, as they brought up the rear of the line and seated themselves about the great table. At a glance, one could readily see that something was different from the ordinary course of events. The air was heavy with the scene of fresh hay, which lay in a thick padding under the table cloth, and in various parts of the large room. Straw was upon the sideboard, straw upon the window-sills, and some was even sprinkled lightly about the highly polished floor, as though dropped carelessly.

The usually gorgeously decorated dining-table was now quite devoid of all ornamentation; not even a bouquet of flowers brightened the centre of the board. Christmas, for Polish families, means fasting and prayer, and not feasting; it is looked upon as a day apart for the observance of religious rites, and to keep before their minds the memory of their Christ and his life of self-denial and goodness.

There was no gayety in the conversation about the table during the meal; all was as solemn and reserved as though some great sorrow had descended upon the family. In almost absolute silence the various courses were brought in and partaken of. Meat was prohibited during this day, but, as if to make up for this deficiency, there were many courses of soups and fish, so that the bill-of-fare was exceedingly lengthy and somewhat tedious.

Not content with serving one kind of soup, there were as many as three upon this occasion, and it was no uncommon thing to serve several more, in very pretentious homes where the head of the house did not consider it unseemly to waste of his plenty. There was a delicious soup made from almonds, then one called barszcz, which was made of fish, and a third made from the juice of beets, which had been allowed to ferment, giving the soup a very sour taste; and, while neither you nor I may care for this sort of broth, yet the Polacks are very fond of it, and have honored it by making it the national soup of the country.

The soup course finished, fish is served. There is tench and pike and carp, besides herring and several kinds of smaller fish, mostly from the great ponds just at the back of the manor-house. It might seem a bit monotonous to eat such quantities of fish at one meal, but each was served with a different kind of gravy or sauce, which quite changed the taste of the dish. Besides, there were vegetables which accompanied them, each differing from the other with each course: mushrooms, and lettuce and cabbages. Plebeian as it may sound to the ears of American children, who are brought up in such a luxuriant manner, the cabbage is a great factor in Polish menus; not being confined to the tables of the poor alone, either.

Salads are now served, with crisp lettuce or water-cress, and a most delicious dish known as "kutia," which is made from oats and honey with poppy seeds added, to give it zest. This is the national dish of the Lithuanians, who have annexed their province to that of Poland.

At last we have arrived at the dessert; but, as puddings and pies are unknown upon the Continent, dessert, or "sweets," as the Polacks call it, consists of fruit, both uncooked and conserved, and a variety of small cakes, or pirogi which are filled with almond paste, or, sometimes, cheese or other toothsome combinations such as poppy seeds, of which the Polacks are very fond.

The meal is finished; the hour draws near that marks the close of day. And now, as a last addition to the feast, the oplatki are broken, each with the other, just as we are accustomed to call out in the wee, small hours of the night, "Merry Christmas," and in this manner do the Polacks wish each other all the compliments of the season.

Mrs. Ostrowska arose from the table first; the children knew full well where she was going, and they eagerly hastened for their heavy wraps and fur caps. Then the little procession filed down the road to the bottom of the hill, merrily singing carols and Christmas hymns, passing from house to house breaking the wafers with the peasants and wishing them all sorts of good things for the coming year. This custom brings master and mistress closer to the tenants, and forms between them a bond of brotherhood.

Mrs. Ostrowska stroked one young girl gently under the chin, as she said:

"This will be your last Christmas under the home-roof, Emilia?"

"I hope so," the girl replied blushingly, as she curtsied and kissed the finger-tips of her patroness. "Francois and I are to be married at the Easter time."

"And then the young sister Helena will find her young man?"

"I hope so," the young girl reiterated.

"We shall be on the lookout for some fine fellow for her," Mrs. Ostrowska said lightly. "There are some very fine young men over to the village at the east of the estate; we must see what we can do," and she moved on, the troop of children at her heels.

Their round of the village over, the whole party returned to the dwór, where they found a servant carrying away the straw which had adorned the dining-hall.

The man stopped as he encountered the mistress of the house, and bowed his head, as if in apology.

"Our cow was taken ill last night, Madame," he explained guiltily. "We thought, perhaps, this might bring her back to health again. We need her milk for the babies. May I?" and he questioned his mistress' face hopefully.

"Take it and welcome," the latter replied kindly, "and may you realize your hopes." Well she knew the superstitions of the peasants in regard to the straw from the Christmas table, which was now supposed to be holy. They had been taught from childhood, and for centuries back from one generation to another had the story been handed down, that this straw possessed remarkable virtues and would not only cure illness in cattle but ward off evil spirits from their homes. It is a harmless delusion, and Mrs. Ostrowska did not interfere in any way with the beliefs of her people. She had even known them to tie the sacred straw about the trunks of the fruit trees, when scale would attack them, and if it chanced that they bore well the following year, they attributed it entirely to the efficacy of the straw.

The younger children were now sent off to bed, while the older ones, with their parents, awaited the hour of Pasterka, or midnight mass.

Service over, in the dim light of early morning, the occupants of the manor made their way slowly homewards on foot. They passed groups of peasant girls, shawls over their heads, loitering on their way to their homes.

"For what are they waiting, mother?" Marya asked, as she noticed that the girls were evidently lingering for an object.

"They are waiting to accost the first young man they meet," the mother replied, "in order to learn his name."

"But what for?" asked Marya a second time.

"That is a peasant custom," the mother answered. "Whatever name is given her, she believes that that will be the name of the man she is destined to marry with. As the girls do not meet with many strangers outside of their own village, it is quite a certainty that they will eventually happen to wed with the one accosted."

"I should like to learn who my future husband will be," the girl said, somewhat in an undertone, scarce daring to voice her wish.

"Marya!" the mother reproved. "What ideas! There is no harm in a peasant girl stopping a stranger on the road upon Christmas Eve; but for you to do so would be unpardonable."

"But I'm a child, mother, too," she persisted, "just as they are children. I don't see any harm in it. It's all in fun, anyway. Please let me," she pleaded, "just this once."

"No, Marya," the mother replied, in a tone of finality. "But you may draw near so as to listen to the girls as they address this young man who approaches around the turn," and the two moved closer toward the knot of village maidens, tittering and giggling among themselves, as they slowly wended their way along the road, half-lingering so that the eligible might overtake them, as if by accident.

"Good evening, sir," the eldest of them said, half timidly, almost afraid of her own boldness, for peasant maidens are modest, "and may I know your name?"

The young man stopped; he swept his fur cap from his head with a lordly air, and replied:

"With pleasure, mademoiselle. Thaddeus."

The village girls tittered; the young man replaced his cap upon his thick hair, and passed on. The "fun" was over until the next "victim" should appear for the next young lady. Every one understands this Christmas Eve custom, and no one would think, even for one instant, of violating its freedom by forcing attention upon the unescorted young girls.

"It wasn't a bit pretty name at all," Marya said. "I'm glad I didn't ask him. I should not like to have my husband's name Thaddeus."

"Don't say that, Marya," the mother reproved gently, "for you know that one of Poland's grandest men was named Thaddeus; Kosciuszco, I mean."

"Yes, mother, I know," the young girl answered; nevertheless she knew it was not a name she would choose for her own particular swain were she able to make her choice. However, she wisely said nothing, but walked briskly along by her mother's side, believing that, perhaps, her mother had been quite right in the matter.

There was very little sleep, if any, for the family the remainder of the night, or rather, morning. No sooner were they arrived at their home and in their beds, than they were awakened by the shouts of the younger children, who pranced about the house in their night-robes in a most injudicious manner. There was music somewhere; some one was singing the kolendy, or Christmas carol. At length the music was discovered to issue from beneath one of the windows in the rear of the house. Pressing their faces against the cold panes, the children saw below them a most wonderful sight. A group of men were singing as they accompanied themselves upon various instruments. Some of them were clad in long, flowing robes, with hair descending upon their shoulders, who represented characters in the Bible, at the time of Christ's life; others wore the aspect of birds, all decked out with gay plumage, and yet another man, the one who wore a golden crown upon his white hair, waved aloft a long wand, upon the very top of which rested a golden star which sparkled in the dim light of the frosty morning.

"THE LITTLE ONES THREW QUANTITIES OF SMALL COINS"

As soon as he saw the children at the windows he held out his hands, into which the little ones threw quantities of small coins begged from their elders. With profound thanks the procession moved on, still singing their kolendy, while the children crept back to their beds, but not to sleep. The Gwiazda, or "Star," had been too much excitement for their little heads, and for full an hour they talked in muffled voices about the wonderful Star of Bethlehem and the queer antics of the men in the cocks' feathers.

Christmas Day dawned; the fasting and penance were finished; merry-making could begin. But, unlike the little American cousin, the Polish cousin does not celebrate Christmas Day with a tree and gifts and romping. It is for him strictly a religious day; there is no gift-giving, these being reserved for his birthdays,which are made occasions for great festivity. And this custom prevails throughout nearly, if not all, the countries in Europe; the birthday is more thought of and celebrated with great gayety than any other holiday in the year.

The day wore on quietly. The older folks sat in the library about the roaring fire and chatted or read, while the younger ones spent their time out of doors, snowballing, sledding and skating.

After luncheon little Jan said:

"Grandfather, you never told me your secret yet, and Christmas Day is almost over."

"What secret?" asked the grandfather, somewhat astonished.

"We know," rang out a small chorus from the older ones.

"Don't you remember what you told me the day I came? You said I should see something wonderful; you told me the name, but I don't remember, it was such a big one."

"Oh, yes," Mr. Ostrowski replied slowly, as he stroked his chin and a merry twinkle came into his eye. "The Jaselki. I had quite forgotten."

"Then we shall not have it," Jan said disappointedly.

"Oh, yes, you shall," his grandfather replied. "It will come just the same. I have already arranged for it. But I wonder what keeps them?" And he pulled out his watch and looked at it.

"The snow is very deep, and the roads bad," Mrs. Ostrowska said, as she looked out of the window toward the avenue of linden trees. "There is no one in sight yet."

"Maybe they won't come," Jan said doubtingly.

"They always do," his grandfather replied. "They haven't missed a single year. But it is only three o'clock; there is plenty of time."

"Will it come by the road?" Jan asked.

"Yes; that is the only way it can come," his grandfather said.

"Then I shall watch," the child said. "When I see them I shall call you."

Jan seated himself at the library window so that he might be able to look far down the wide road leading to the entrance of the park. There was silence for a long time. Then he suddenly called out:

"What will they look like, grandfather?"

"They will come in a covered wagon," Mr. Ostrowski answered.

Silence again. After some little time, Jan called out excitedly:

"I see them; they have just come through the brama."

Such a jumping and scampering as there was then in the great house! There was no holding the children back from running out to the front porch to meet the arrivals. It was indeed a peculiar-looking crowd that made its appearance. A huge wagon, mounted on runners, most gorgeously decorated with tinsel of gold and silver, and covered with strings upon strings of tiny bells, was making its way slowly up the driveway. Had it been a little American child who had seen it, he would at once have remarked that it was a circus-wagon. The sleigh bells jingled merrily; and, as the wagon pulled up at the entrance of the manor, the driver smiled pleasantly at the children's welcome. He knew Peter and Marya well, for he had come every year to their home upon Christmas Day to present his plays. He nodded to them and wished them a happy Christmastide; he bowed respectfully to the other children, with whom he was unacquainted, for he considered all children as his own peculiar property.

Before the wondering eyes of the excited children, the driver and his assistants set up the show. They watched them, with wide-opened eyes, light the numberless small candles about the stage arch; the gold and silver tinsel now sparkled out like a miniature fairy-land. The old horse would look around every little while, as though trained to do so, to see that everything was being done in an approved manner. This set the strings of bells to vibrating, so that their melody rang out over the snow, attracting the attention of the peasants in the village beyond, who promptly gathered to witness the exhibition.

Jaselki means a manger; and because these travelling showmen give scenes from the life of Christ they are called jaselki, or manger-men. For over an hour the children, not to mention the grown folks, were fascinated by the miracle-play. Then, the entertainment over, the men were ushered into the servants' quarters, where they received warm food and drink, after which they packed up their wagon and departed for Cracow, where they were to give more representations during the evening upon the rynek, or public square.

It is only at Christmas that these plays are given; during other seasons of the year these showmen present other sorts of entertainments, so that from one year's end to the other, they travel about in their gorgeously decorated wagons, sometimes on wheels, sometimes on runners, living in the open air, the life of nomads. Christmas Day is over. Night descends and quiet reigns at the dwór. The great house is early wrapped in slumber, and thus ends the holiday season.

CHAPTER V

THE VISIT TO THE GAILY PAINTED COTTAGE

A DAY or two later, the guests departed, and the Ostrowski family took up its daily routine. The boy Peter resumed his studies under the care and instruction of his tutor, while the little Marya returned to the guidance of her governess, for each child in a wealthy family in Poland has his or her own tutor or tutoress. Child life in upper circles is quite a thing apart from the lives of the grown-ups. Their hours are widely different; they dress simply and live simply, receiving instruction in the arts and languages; the girls to be fine housekeepers and womanly; the boys to be courteous, manly and well versed in those matters which pertain to the care and interest of the estate which is later to devolve upon their shoulders.

Mrs. Ostrowska never breakfasted with her children. She rose about eleven o'clock, had her morning meal in her own rooms, and after tending to her household duties, devoted the better part of the afternoon to the needs of her peasantry. She was a very charitable woman, as are all the upper-class Polacks, and devoted many hours among these people. She had sewing classes for the young girls, where they were taught to do, not only the plain sewing necessary for their own use, but embroidery of the most exquisite kind, so that they might employ their idle moments, during the long, cold winter days, in making articles to sell in the cities. Furthermore, she established cooking classes; she aided the sick; and doctors being very far away, the mistress of the manor was usually called upon in case of illness among the peasantry; even the children were taught that most useful and beneficial branch of science, first aid to the injured. Were it not for the generosity and far-sightedness of the landed proprietors in looking after the interests and education of these peasants, there would be most abject poverty and suffering among them.

The Ostrowski estate is one of the oldest in Poland; it numbers fully four hundred thousand acres; and, in order to grasp the immensity of this, you must know that one ordinary city block measures five acres, so that it would require about six hundred and twenty-five blocks each way to cover

28

this enormous estate. And you may be quite certain, it is no small task to properly look after and make profitable an estate of this size.

There is a distillery which distils spirits from the potatoes raised upon one portion of the estate; there is a sugar refinery, which transforms the juicy red beets into snowy white sugar; there are cotton-mills, which are kept going by the thousands of bales of soft, fluffy cotton grown upon the place; there are endless factories and mills of every description, all under the care of the master of the manor. He would much prefer not to add these industries to his business cares, but he is a charitable man; he knows that to every rich man there are thousands of poor. If the beets and the potatoes, the grain and the cotton were allowed to go out in their raw state, for manufacture elsewhere, there would be many workmen thrown out of employment. Perhaps these same poor might be compelled to seek their fortunes in our own beloved land, and this would mean the loss of many valuable citizens, who will be wanted some day, to stand up for Poland and help her win back her lost liberty. Therefore, Mr. Ostrowski, having a clear head, decided to use his products upon his land, and, in this way, he gave employment to thousands of families, for not only were the men put to work at the heavier tasks, but the women helped out with the spinning and the lighter tasks.

The villages attached to the Ostrowski estate are model ones. They are naturally situated at great distances apart, each village clustering itself about the particular factory near by. The huts nestle snugly at the foot of the hill upon which stands the dwór, as if they craved protection from their superior. In groups of two and threes they huddle together, these low-roofed, whitewashed, plastered houses, a door in the centre, a window at either side affording scant light to the two rooms within. The European peasants seem greatly to object to admitting light into their home; perhaps it is but the lingering custom of barbaric days when man feared to present an entrance into his sacred precincts to a possible enemy; perhaps it is but the relic of an ancient law, but recently repealed in France, that every opening, be it door or window, giving upon the street or road, is taxed; and if there is one bugbear in the vocabulary of the peasant, it is "taxes."

A bit of a garden lies in front of each home, while at the rear is the truck garden, where enough vegetables are raised to last during the winter season. Some of the more prosperous tenants possess a cow, or a pig, or perhaps even a goose; nevertheless, whatever the size of the family, brute and otherwise, they all live in harmony and happiness together in the two low-ceiled rooms. The roof of thatch, covered with its thick coating of mud, moss-grown, tones the scene to one of great picturesqueness, as seen from the distance.

Toward one of these huts Mrs. Ostrowska bent her steps this bright, sunny morning in early January. It was much like all the other huts in the village, but infinitely gayer. Over the doors and windows were broad bands of red and blue and yellow painted with a rude hand, with dabs of triangles and other geometrical forms. There were all sorts of attempts at decoration. Mrs. Ostrowska smiled as she viewed the fresh colors, and knocked loudly at the heavy wooden door.

It was opened by an elderly woman, whose gray hair fell carelessly from its loose coil upon her head. She was greatly surprised to see the mistress of the manor, but motioned her graciously to enter.

"Good morning," Mrs. Ostrowska said, as she stepped into the smoky atmosphere of the room, "and how do you find yourself this morning, Mrs. Gadenz?"

"Oh, very well, thank you, Madame, except that the little Henryk is not so well; his cough is worse."

"I must have the doctor look after him when he makes his rounds," the mistress answered. Then she added, "I see by the decorationsupon your home that Helena is to be allowed to receive visits from the young men. Any prospects of a husband yet?"

"No," the woman replied. "Thad put the colors on just before Christmas, so there hasn't been much time for the young men to know that Helena is old enough to have callers. Now that Emilia is to be married at the Easter time, we thought it better to get her sister started."

"She isn't fifteen yet, is she?"

"No," answered the peasant, "but then there are so many of us we must not keep them all at home. Some must make way for the younger ones. I did it, and my daughters must do so, too."

"You were married very young, were you not?" Mrs. Ostrowska asked kindly, not meaning to be inquisitive, but Mrs. Gadenz was a comparative stranger upon the estate; that is, she was not born there, as so many of the other peasants had been; she had come with her husband and small children from other parts to find work in the distillery of Mr. Ostrowski.

"At thirteen," the peasant woman replied proudly.

She was now in her thirty-eighth year, although she appeared much older; taking up her wifely burdens at such a tender age, so common to the peasants of Poland, had made her seem much older. But despite her faded cheeks and hair fast turning gray, she was strong and active, and the fire of the Slav still shone in her eye.

The three or four younger children, ranging from ten to three, were playing upon the floor, tumbling one another about over the cat and her kittens, and frolicking with the shaggy-coated dog, who was monopolizing the warmest corner of the great stove.

"Be quiet, children," the mother spoke sharply, as she reproved the boisterous youngsters. "Don't you know that the lady of the manor is here?"

"Let them play," the lady interposed, "they get but little of it, at best."

Meanwhile, Emilia had left her duty of stirring the porridge on the great plaster stove and withdrawn into the only other room. In a moment she returned, followed by the younger sister, who approached the mistress of the dwór and respectfully kissed her hand.

"I wish to be the first to congratulate you," the great lady said, "upon being out in the world now. You are, indeed, growing to be quite a young lady. Not yet fifteen, and waiting for a lover. I want you to come up to the manor Thursday afternoon with Emilia. I have some sewing for you, and perhaps we shall be able to fill out that linen chest so that you may find a most superior husband."

The young girl blushed and thanked her benefactress kindly, promising to be on hand promptly. Then she retired to the next room to finish her tasks there.

"I'm glad to see you so housewifely," Mrs. Ostrowska said, as she watched the young Emilia move about the room, stirring the great pot of porridge one moment, while in the next she was tending to the little wants of the younger ones. "Jan will have need of a good cook."

Emilia blushed deeply and her face brightened up; into her soft blue eyes came a look of tenderness, for was she not thinking of her own dear one, beloved Jan, to whom she was to be married at the Easter-tide? And these latter days she was indeed busy with the last preparations; there was much left to do, for she herself was to make the wedding gown.

"You will be glad to have your own little home, Emilia?" the lady queried kindly.

"Yes," came the quick reply. "There are so many of us, and the house is very crowded. It will be far better when I have a home of my own."

Emilia set the iron pot on the back of the stove, where its contents might keep warm until the visitor had departed, when the children might then have their midday meal. She turned to still the whimpering of the little child in the far corner, stretched upon the straw, the child with the cough.

"You are nearly ready for the wedding day?" continued the interlocutor of the young girl, as the latter stooped to pick up the child and hold him in her lap.

"Almost. There is yet the wedding gown to make, besides some small household things not quite ready. Oh, how I wish the day would hasten!" she added, with a long-drawn sigh, drawing the young child's fair head closer to her breast and pressing a warm, tender kiss upon the glossy curls.

Mrs. Ostrowska could understand why. She regarded the young girl carefully. She knew that the poor have very few pleasures, that the older must always care for the younger, and that young girls crave merriment and company. With a house full of young children, the mother away all day in the mills or the fields, it devolved upon her, the eldest, to manage the little household, to hush the sobs of the offended baby, or bind up a hurt finger; she it was who prepared the meals for the many mouths, who washed the few necessary articles of apparel, and the common every-day round of family cares was distasteful to her simply because she had no recreations interspersed among them, for we all know the old adage, "All work and no play makes Jack a dull boy." Mrs. Ostrowska understood very well the wants of her people; it was for this reason she came among them every day; seeing an opportunity here to lighten the burden of one young girl, or helping a talented young boy to gain instruction in the art or trade that appealed to him. She was attempting to teach her peasantry that each one should be given the chance for which he so longed; and that he should not be brought up to follow such and such a calling simply because his father had followed the same calling from boyhood, which he, in turn, had followed after his father.

The elder peasants sometimes resented this interference in their family affairs, as they were sometimes wont to call it, in moments of peevishness, but Mrs. Ostrowska did her good work quietly and unostentatiously; she helped the marriageable girls fill their linen chests, which somewhat ameliorated the feelings of the elders toward her, for it meant a saving of much expense to them; she introduced social etiquette in her sewing circles on Friday mornings; she taught the valuable science of aiding the sick and injured so that there should be less illness among the poor; for rather than spend their hard-earned pence for medical services they will suffer uncomplainingly. Furthermore, she was slowly making progress in instilling into them the need and benefits of sanitation in their homes.

Every week Mr. Ostrowski made the rounds of his estate on horseback, to inspect the cottages which he took such pride in; he argued with the tenants to compel them to maintain these homes in cleanliness; for it is a difficult matter to keep things ship-shape when a dozen or more often occupy two or three rooms, to make no mention of the four-footed occupants, or the feathered tribe.

"I want you to come up to the dwór Thursday afternoon with Helena," Mrs. Ostrowska said, after a long silence. "You can begin your gown then, and you two sisters can work together."

"I should love to," the young girl replied, as her face brightened. She was glad of the opportunity to get away from the confinement of the hut and the household duties for a short time, and this meant an afternoon of extreme pleasure for her. All the peasant girls loved to be invited to the manor, for a cup of warm, delicious tea served with lemon, and pirogi, those most delectable cakes filled with almond meal which were such luxuries to them, awaited them.

"I have a woman coming from Cracow," Mrs. Ostrowska continued, as she rose to leave, "who is bringing some very pretty little trinkets from the city. I should like to have you there to make a selection of such as you would care to have."

"You are more than kind," the girl replied, in a low voice. "You are always thinking of our pleasure and happiness."

"That is my duty," the older woman answered; "you are all my children, and I must give you as much happiness as I can, for some day you will be beyond my care and protection, and will have no one but your Jan to look after you."

Again the girl blushed a deep red, and the tender look returned to her soft eyes at the mention of her fiancé. She escorted her patroness to the door of the cottage and closed it after her. Then she resumed her tasks about the kitchen, giving the little ones their meal of barszcz and a slice cut from a cake of cabbage which had been pressed into a solid loaf.

Mrs. Ostrowska was glad to be in the clear, crisp air once more, after the stifling atmosphere of the cottage, for her peasants were slow to learn the value of ventilation. As she continued her way down the road toward the manor-house, she thought of her "young people," as she called them fondly, for she took a personal interest in each of them, whether large or small, girl or boy.

She reviewed their lives, as they live them from one generation to the other. How they roll and toss upon the floor of their cabins or upon the greensward, in unconscious bliss of childhood. How they attain the age of youth when they must begin to help share the burdens of the elders either in the fields or the mills, if they be boys, or in spinning and caring for the helpless ones at home, if they be girls. How they grow up to manhood and womanhood with very little time for pleasures and holidays, for all hands must take hold that the weight may not fall upon one. How finally, the young girls attain the age of fifteen or more, when they are allowed to consider the question of marriage. Then comes to them courters, and love enters into their lives, to brighten the eye and redden the cheek. They live for months and months upon the delights they will experience in attending church, the wedding procession, and the carrying-off of the bride; then the settling down in their own nests. After that, they are no longer helpers in the household, they are the mainstays of their own homes, and they realize then what it really means to be home-makers. They take up their cares and their duties; they arise early, but then, they have always been used to that; they must spin and knit, and sew and darn, and there are no other fingers to help them. For many years they must do all, until the little fingers are big enough and strong enough to aid. Sometimes, they must go out into the forest and gather fagots for their fires so that the little one may not suffer from the chill; they must learn the wonderful art of making a few pence do duty of many. And year by year passes; they see their daughters grow up to that age when they, in turn, must leave their homes for homes of their own; they see their sons going away to the army or to other lands, perhaps, to seek their fortunes; and thus, from generation to generation, they continue in this routine, living in memory, throughout those days when their lives are filled with busy cares, that day, so long ago, when they drove to the village church, the bridal veil falling about their slender shoulders, the wedding supper and the gay dance, and the clamor of voices as they rolled away with their loved ones in the village cart for the honeymoon. And all the burdens of their lives, all the toil, all the care and the endless sameness are more than compensated for by that one glorious day of their existence — their wedding day.

Mrs. Ostrowska planned and planned how she could educate these peasants in such wise as to fit them for more than mere care-takers; that they might learn a little of the refinements of life, and that, by education, they might gradually raise themselves to a higher andbetter plane. Her work was slow, but she felt that already she could see signs of having accomplished something material of betterment in their lives.

CHAPTER VI

CARNIVAL SEASON

JANUARY has passed, and February is ushered in with the Feast of the Candles, or Candlemas Day, which takes place upon the second day of the month. This is one of the most devout religious celebrations in the land, for the peasants believe, were they to forget this ceremony even once, that their villages would be devastated by the wolves which prowl about over the plains in search of food when the ground is covered thick with snow, and it is difficult for them to find sustenance. Long years before, the villages were not as frequent, nor as well protected as they now are; therefore, it did happen that the wild beasts would descend in droves upon the homes of these poor people, who were powerless to drive them away. Sometimes, these voracious animals would even carry off the peasants' children before their very eyes. Consequently, as the peasants were unable to cope with the enemy, they must seek assistance somewhere, and where more naturally than of their patron saint? This chanced to be the good St. Michael; but even he was at times without sufficient power to repel the advances of these beasts. Therefore, with one accord, the villagers banded together and made a vow to offer up their prayers to the Virgin Mother. They pleaded with her, on bended knees, in the village church, to ward off this dread enemy and to send them protection. Whether the prayer was effective or not is a question. But the story goes that the Holy Mother seized a lighted candle in her hand, and holding it in such a manner as to send the bright flame in the faces of the animals that preyed at the very borders of the village, so frightened them that they turned tail and fled, leaving the peasants in peace and security, for wild beasts do not take kindly to fire. It was because they were so miraculously saved from this dreadful menace that the people thenceforth celebrated the day each year, which is known as the Gromnice. And to-day, when they hear the familiar voices of their tormentor in the far distance of the woods, they mutter in their half-waking sleep, "In Thy care, O Mary," and they leave the rest of the responsibility to their intercessor.

"THE PROCESSION FORMED, THE MARCH BEGINS TO THE CHURCH"

Early in the morning of the second of February, the peasants begin to congregate in the village square, which is the usual meeting place on all occasions of public demonstration. Each one, whether he be an old, bowed man or a tiny tot just able to stand, holds in his hand a candle, whose light falls upon his face all lit up with religious fervor. The procession formed, the march begins to the church, the oldest leading.

It is not the custom of European churches to provide pews for the worshippers; consequently, unless one is able to afford the luxury of a low-seated chair upon which to kneel, for the chairs are never used to sit upon, he must content himself with kneeling upon the hard, cold stone floor. It is truly an imposing sight to see the tall aisle of the church lighted by the flicker of hundreds of candles, the peasants, in their vari-colored garments, kneeling devoutly upon the floor, heads bowed. It is very real to them, this service for their deliverance from the fangs of the wolf; and so strong is their faith that they even place the blessed candles, after the ceremony is finished, safely away in some treasured chest or upon their own private altar, that they may serve them in time of sickness, trouble or any calamity.

But woe betide the one whose candle blows out! Evil is certain to follow in his footsteps; from that moment, he believes himself a doomed man. Should it prove to be the candle of a young girl, perhaps one upon the verge of her wedding day, it would instantly throw her into hysterics, for she would know to a certainty that she will never get a husband. And what a disgrace she would be in the eyes of the whole village! A girl without a husband, an "old maid," as commonly known in our parlance, would be an unpardonable offence to the relatives, who would look askance at her, so strongly is the idea of marriage imparted to them. It is quite as much of a disgrace for a woman to remain unmarried, among the Polish peasantry, as it is for a man to have no home of his own. When a Polish peasant dies, he usually leaves behind him a small bit of ground, upon which stands his cottage with its tiny garden-space. This is partitioned equally among the man's children, be they many or few.

But all men are not fortunate. It sometimes happens that illness will rob a man of his little he has saved during his years of toil, or careless habits, perhaps, will dwindle his patrimony to almost nothing, so that when at last he leaves this world, he has nothing which may be divided among his children. But the peasants do not take these matters into consideration at all. They have one code and they can see no other way of looking at things. If a child has been willed no patrimony, then he must get one of his own, for he is looked down upon as thoroughly worthless who is compelled to find lodgings in the home of a stranger. These men are known as kormorniki, from the word komora, meaning room. In Poland a kormorniki has about the same reputation among his companions as a tramp has among respectable people in America.

After Candlemas Day comes the Carnival week, which is the week, as you all know, preceding Lent. As a final respite before theforty days of fasting and prayer which will follow so soon, the people allow themselves all sorts of liberties and gayeties. Balls are given, "hunts" are on, and joy reigns supreme, not only in the city, but in the remote country places.

Again the manor-house is alive with brilliant lights and many faces. The owners of adjoining estates, with their wives and grown-up sons and daughters, friends of the family, from quite remote parts even, are gathered together for one week of holidays. It is a pleasure to see such wit and beauty gathered together under one roof; for Polish women are almost all handsome, with their soft eyes, their beautiful complexions and their glossy, dark hair. Their manners are a marvel, and their bearing graceful and easy. They are capital company and well informed on all the topics of the day, so that conversation never lags, nor are they obliged to fall back upon the inevitable "cards" for amusement. With them the art of conversation has not died out, nor the art of entertaining.

The snow lay thick upon the ground; the branches of the tall fir trees were clothed in a heavy coating of whiteness. The sky overhead was a dull, leaden color; but the guests at the manor-house were pleased with the wintry conditions, for it but aided them in the "hunt" that was "on" that morning.

Breakfast finished, a hearty affair of meat, cheese and beverages of various sorts, the sleighs drew up to the portico with boisterous jangling of sleigh-bells and champing of horses' bits; the thoroughbred animals pawing in impatience to be off in the crisp, frosty air. Gay with red tassels, which swept the front dash of the heavy sleighs, and joyful with the chime of the tiny bells, the party drove off to the neighboring woods, where lay, in unconscious innocence of their fate, the fleet deer. The chill of the winter's morning did not affect the spirits of the party in any degree, for they were all snugly wrapped in thick fur robes, and large fur caps completely swathed their heads, so that nothing visible remained of them but their vivacious eyes and their ruddy noses.

Along the broad road the sleighs sped, in single file, past the peasant village around the bend of the hill, and off toward the forest stretching miles ahead of them, the tall tops of the trees nodding a "good morning" to them as they approached. Among the firs and oaks the sleighs were soon lost to sight, winding in and out among the dark trees until the wagon-road came abruptly to an end and only a path stretched in front. It was but the work of a few moments to clear a considerable circle, and light the huge bonfire around which every one gathered, stretching out their half-benumbed hands. Such a chattering and rumpus! Instead of grown-ups, you might have imagined them to be a bunch of school-children just out for recess. But Polish aristocracy understand how to enjoy themselves under all conditions.

Not long did they tarry about the camp-fire. It was not for this they had taken the long, chilly drive. Gathering together their equipment, and shouldering their guns, off they tramped through the heavy underbrush; only a few of the more delicate ladies remained by the warmth of the cheery flame.

Slowly, slowly they made their way cautiously, until they came within sight of the tiny tracks, for the freshly fallen snow was a sorry telltale for the "game."

Shivering, but happy under their load of game, the party returned a couple of hours later, to find everything prepared for the ensuing meal. The great iron pot hung steaming over the glowing coals, the aroma of something therein greeting their nostrils with delight. For all were famished and in good mood to enjoy a camp dinner. It seemed but a matter of a few minutes before the cook and his assistants had the game ready for the steaming sauce which awaited it in the iron pot; and while the company regaled themselves with jokes and talk of the day's sport, the sauce bubbled and boiled, but tantalizing the group about the fire. However, all things come to those who wait, and it really was not such a great wait before they were all "falling-to" with keen appetites. The cuisine was excellent, and the gamey meat had a relish all its own.

But now the party must hasten home. Too long have they lingered among the pine trees, and much longer yet could they tarry, were there not other arrangements for the evening. But dinner was awaiting them at the dwór; and at nine o'clock, as the dining-hall filled with the gay company, in evening dress, you scarce would have recognized them as the same persons who had gathered about the camp-fire among the pine trees but a few hours previously.

There is always time for everything in Poland, for the rich. The dinner lengthened itself out until well toward eleven o'clock. Then came the "grand ball," for this is Ash Wednesday, the last day of gayety before the Lenten season begins.

What a delight it is to watch the Polish men and women dance! It comes naturally to them, and I really believe they would much prefer dancing to any other occupation. While the manor-folks confine themselves to the more conventional forms of the dance, down in the village the peasants dance to the wild mazurkas and sing weird folk-songs. But in hut or mansion, there is gayety abroad this last night of freedom; a short hour, and then, Lent, fasting, prayer for forty days, observed in most rigorous manner.

Forty days, nearly six weeks, pass after all, and before the Lenten days are two-thirds over, preparations are already begun for the Easter day. Those indeed are busy times in the culinary quarters at the dwór. Such heaps and heaps of food as are prepared in the great kitchens! Such stacks and stacks of bread as are baked in the huge ovens, so different from our own cook-stoves. Gas stoves are unknown in Poland; all the ovens are brick affairs, such as are used by bakers, in to which great logs of heavy wood are placed. And, when the bricks have been heated to the degree necessary for the food which is to be cooked, the fire is withdrawn by long rakes of iron and this heat is retained for a long enough time to bake.

The Saturday before Easter the table is set in the long dining-room. This table presents quite a different appearance from that of the Christmas table. Now there is every sort of decoration one could wish for. Hot-house flowers everywhere; colored Easter eggs, just as we have, fruit, and sugar lambs. We American folks can scarce conceive of such lavishness in articles of food. Not only is there a young pig served whole upon a gayly decorated platter, but there are, at intervals the length of the great table, immense roasts of all kinds; hams with accompanying sauces, beef, mutton, and not even the "sweets" are forgotten.

All being in readiness, the village priest enters and places his blessing upon the food which graces the groaning board. This is really quite a serious custom, this blessing of the food, the houses and everything that pertains to existence. The peasants are most superstitious in this, and would no more dare to enter a new home or even a theatre which had not received this blessing at the hands of the priest or bishop, than they would purposely run into danger.

Easter day itself is quiet. There is the heavy dinner in the early part of the day, when Easter wishes are bestowed upon one and all, even the giving of Easter eggs, as we do, not being omitted.

And now dawns Easter Monday. The religious ceremonies are finished; the Sabbath has passed, and on Monday may begin the merry-making once more. The Polacks are very fond of life and merriment. They take advantage of every occasion upon which to indulge in relaxation from work, and always, in a quiet way, they get the most out of living that is possible. Just as we celebrate Hallowe'en with pranks and games, so the Polacks celebrate the Smigus on Easter Monday. Among the peasantry, the jokes are a trifle rougher than in upper circles, but they are always good-natured, and never do they allow themselves to overstep, even in the slightest degree. The Smigus is, indeed, a merry romp.

Watch this jaunty little chap as he whistles gayly on his way to the home of his adored one. Much courage does it take to venture forth such a night as this. But when one goes to visit her, he cares not; he is only too proud to display his courage, for will not she love him the better for it? Swish! The whistling is stopped. A series of muffled sounds, and the young man regains his equilibrium once again. He journeys on, but not quite so merrily. His teeth chatter just a little in his head, and he walks a trifle quicker. For the water was cold, and it is not very comfortable to be drenched unawares. Nevertheless, he feels himself more or less of a martyr for her sake, and he carries his head high with self-satisfied pride.

And hark! There is tittering somewhere. Now we can trace it to the village well. Let us go and enjoy the sport. My, but what a screaming! It fairly makes one's ears tingle. We hasten our steps, for we know there are girls mixed up in this affair; their shrill, nervous voices proclaim it upon the still, clear air of the night. As Helena and her two young friends from across the road were making their way to the public well, they, too, were drenched in exactly the same manner as the young man had been but a moment before. But, then, Helena and her friends should have known better than to venture out upon Easter Monday evening. Who can say but that they rather enjoyed the experience? However, they had their reward, for the young gallants, good-hearted men if somewhat rough, filled the pitchers for the maidens and carried them to the doors of their homes upon their own stout shoulders. And they all laughed heartily at the joke. Perhaps, who knows, but that they might meet their future husbands here?

While the peasants amuse themselves in these harmless, jolly pranks, the occupants of the dwór enjoy similar ones, but somewhat differently. There, the young men are more courtly. Catching their prey unawares, they shower her with delicate cologne-water, or twine gayly colored ribbons about her neck, making her their captive. And thus, in hut and manor-house, passes Easter Monday.

But you must not believe that the sports are all confined to the country-side. Indeed not. The city folks have their own form of entertainment, and in the City of Cracow there is observed a most peculiar custom known as Renkawka or the Sleeve.

In very olden times, I believe about the year 560 A. D., there lived in the south, among the Carpathian Mountains, a very unimportant chief named Krakus. He was a good man, a most unusual thing in that age; therefore everybody loved him, and that was a great honor, because the times were warlike and people cared more for a chief who showed himself brave but fierce than they did about one whowas gentle and kind. It so happened that Krakus made a journey to the north. He came to a fine hill, about whose foot ran a broad, clear river called the Vistula. As he was looking for a site upon which to build himself a fortress, he decided this was just the very place for his. But he found it one thing to wish and quite another thing to obtain. The hill was guarded by a fierce dragon who kept watch, day and night, that no one might take it away. However, Krakus was a brave man, and he longed so intensely for the hill, especially now that he knew he ought not to have it, that he decided to fight the dreadful dragon. Therefore, he took his trusty sword and shield, mounted the hill, fought the monster and conquered it. Had he not done so, there would have been no story. He then set to work to build his castle upon the very top of that impregnable hill, with the beautiful river running around its base. He called the fortress-castle the Wawel, because that was the name of the hill upon which it stood.

This castle of Krakus still is standing, but it is in a sad state of ruin. However, the Russian government, to whom it now belongs, is putting it in repair, so that it may present the same appearance of grandeur and splendor that it did in the days of good King Krakus.

You all know what a castle is; but perhaps there are few of you who understand what it means when applied to an ancient stronghold. The Wawel castle really included quite a small village inside its massive walls, for here the chief or king, with his retainers and his army, were wont to lock themselves safely in at close of day, that the enemy, who was always lurking in wait in those times, could do them no harm. It is here, to this Wawel, that Mrs. Ostrowska had promised to take the children in the June time, upon St. John's Eve, to witness the ceremony of the Wianki.

Now, when King Krakus died, his people mourned him exceedingly. They erected a huge mound outside the city on the further side of the river in his honor. The peasants wore a sort of tunic, at that time, with very wide sleeves, much like the sleeves worn by Japanese women. It was in these convenient sleeves they carried the earth with which to erect the mound, hence the ceremony takes its name Renkawka or Sleeve.

It is a peculiarity of the Polish peasant that, once a custom is established, it is never abandoned, even though the necessity has long since passed away. I doubt very much if any of those who participate in the Renkawka could tell you why the custom is observed; nevertheless each Easter Monday they gather about the mound, dressed in these old-fashioned garments with wide sleeves. They no longer carry earth with them, as in the old days, however; they bring nothing, but they return with full sleeves, for it has developed into a custom for the rich to send the food which has been left from the Easter feast, that it might be distributed among the needy.

CHAPTER VII

THE VILLAGE WEDDING

SOME few days after Easter, while the children at the dwór were reading to their mother in the library, the clatter of hoofs was heard upon the hard road without. Marya jumped up from her chair and ran, with fleet steps, to the front window overlooking the entrance-porch. Such a clatter and racket as there was! One would almost imagine himself back in the days of post-horses and outriders. There, under cover of the carriage entrance, were four gayly dressed young peasants, proudly seated upon slick horses, who were stamping their feet and neighing most strenuously.

"Mother," cried Marya excitedly, "see what's here! Quick!"

Mrs. Ostrowska smiled, but did not hasten, for she well knew the meaning of this hubbub. This was the formal invitation to the krakowich, the wedding of Emilia. She approached the French window and stepped out upon the wide veranda, and she smiled a welcome to the druzbowie, who had come to extend their best wishes from the bride and the groom, and all their relatives, to the mistress and master of the manor, together with their family and their guests, and to request their presence at the wedding of the fair Emilia at the village church at noon.

After Mrs. Ostrowska assured the best men of their acceptance and that they all would be most pleased to accept the kind invitation, the four young men rode gayly down the sloping driveway and disappeared at the bend of the road, their gorgeous feathers flowing free in the breeze. And only the clatter of their horses' feet were heard in the distance.

In great state, the family coach drew up to the entrance-porch some time later and the Ostrowski family drove off toward the home of the bride. It seemed as though the entire populace had turned out for the occasion. Such a crowd as there was gathered before the tiny home! And such colors! And yet more people pouring out of the one small door of the humble cottage. One would scarce believe it possible for so small a space to hold so many persons! But no one asks or wishes much room upon such a festal occasion as this; and there was nothing but smiling faces, bright eyes, and gay colors to be seen.

One wondered, too, where the simple peasant girls could have obtained such gorgeous raiment. There were black velvet gowns, all tight-fitting, with short sleeves, and ankle length. Some were exquisitely embroidered in gold or silver thread, others in bright silks, or even in colored cotton thread. But there was every conceivable hue and shade. If they have nothing else, these peasant maidens will have a holiday attire of the most gorgeous, and they take delight and pride in saving up for years in order to make their own costumes more beautiful than their neighbors'. Over their dark, glossy hair a brilliant handkerchief is knotted, one in one manner, one in another, but all of them picturesque. It would seem impossible for the Polish peasant to be other than charming in her holiday dress.

"SHE WAS BUNDLED INTO THE VILLAGE CART"

Some of the more fortunate ones wore long pendants from their brown ears, while yet others had on long strings of beads, some of coral, others of pearls, or yet of a bluish stone resembling turquoise. Every bit of finery, some handed down from one generation to another, priceless treasures, was in evidence upon this occasion, and even the young men were scarce outdone in their velvet jackets and gay sashes.

The occupants of the carriage from the manor-house saluted the assembled peasants warmly, who returned their salute. Marya looked in vain for the young bride; she was nowhere to be seen. But Helena, the younger sister, approached and offered the master and mistress a drink in which to toast her sister.

At length Marya spied her; she was just issuing forth from the cottage-door. Her white veil fell over her young shoulder with grace as she made her way slowly to the carriage in order to receive the blessing of her master and mistress. Suddenly, kneeling in respect, the bride was seized by several burly men in gala attire. With a scream of terror, and amid copious tears, all of which were part of the programme, she was bundled into the village cart and the procession moved onwards, headed by two of the best men, while the other two druzbowie brought up the rear to escort the bridal couple to the church. This is one of the pretty customs left of the old days when the grooms were in the habit of virtually and truly stealing away their brides before the very eyes of their fond parents, often without the consent of the young lady herself. It is a harmless practice at this day, and a pretty one, affording much pleasure to the bride, and much satisfaction to the groom. Besides, the peasants would scarce believe themselves properly married unless this ceremony prevailed.

The longest part of a wedding is not at the church; the service lasted but a very short time when every one wended his way back to the home of the bride once again. During their absence the tables had been laid for the wedding supper, supplied by the generosity of the master of the dwór, and then having drank a last health to the young couple, the rooms were cleared for the wedding dance.

The village had not seen such a wedding for many years as Emilia had. She was a general favorite, with her quiet manners, her soft voice and her kind ways to all.

After the grand march, led by the bride, who leaned upon the arm of Mr. Ostrowski himself, followed by the groom with Mrs. Ostrowska, the master and mistress withdrew from the scene, leaving the peasants to enjoy the dancing and gayety to their hearts' content without the consequent restraint of their presence.

Now, indeed, did the stout old walls of the plastered hut ring with merriment! The beams fairly shook under the heavy tread of so many husky feet, and it was not until a late hour of the afternoon that the bride and her husband were able to make their escape.

Until every ceremony has been gone through with, the young Polish peasant bride may not free herself from the attentions of the four best men, who take it upon themselves to act as a sort of body-guard and chaperones. Therefore, under their protection, the newly-wedsrepaired to the top of the hill for their final blessing, as well, no doubt, as a substantial wedding gift.

The day for them was about finished. The visit to the village photographer was the end; here they were photographed in all the finery of their wedding dress, the one leaning lovingly upon the arm of the other; and what a comfort it will be to them, in the years that are to come, when trials and tribulations come to them, to look upon the picture of themselves as they were upon that delightful day of their wedding, young, care-free and happy.

And thus the wedding day of Emilia drew to a close.

There was one very amusing incident which occurred at the wedding, but not at all out of the ordinary among the Polish peasantry. Necessarily, being poor, they economize in those things which are not absolute necessities; and shoes being one of these, they are in thehabit of going barefoot. But they always possess one pair of best shoes, usually with very high French heels, of which they are inordinately proud. It would amount almost to sacrilege for them to wear these creations on any but the grandest and most important occasions. It would be a pity to scuff them out upon the dusty, rocky roads; so, as the women made their way to the church, they carried their shoes and put them on at the entrance of the church. I really believe they did this more because they would be unable to walk in such high-heeled affairs, for it is somewhat of an art to manage one's feet properly, even at best. As soon as the occasion was over, the shoes were laid carefully aside for use upon another gala day. In this way, one pair of shoes will last a life-time, and no doubt many of them descend to the younger members of the family, as the older ones outgrow them.

And now the weeks are speeding by, and Corpus Christi Day has come, a religious festival which takes place about eight weeks after Easter. It is a national holiday, and in the city of Cracow the procession Bozé Cialo takes place. Here, in the rynek, or public square, gather the entire population of the city, from the oldest infirm inhabitant to the youngest toddler each with his candle in his hand. The bishop of the church conducts the ceremony of the day with great solemnity; and the procession marches around the great square with banners and images of the Christ, while little flower girls, crowned with white flowers, scatter rose-petals from the dainty baskets hung from their shoulders. The soldiers, with their bright uniforms and their gay helmets, mingle with the worshippers, and all is bustle, light and solemnity. After the ceremony, however, the crowds disperse to make merry during the remainder of the day; for in Europe, upon fast days, after the religious services are ended, the people are at liberty to enjoy themselves as they best care to.

Spring has truly arrived; the leaves are budding forth now in all their new greenness. The spring flowers are shooting forth from their winter shelter and the sun shines warmly, but the air is yet a trifle crisp.

There has been a general house-cleaning during the past few days among the Polish peasantry, just as we have a general house-cleaning time, so much dreaded by our fathers. The huts in the villages have been freshly whitewashed; some, even, have been tinted blue to vary the monotony. About the doors and windows are bound great boughs of green, for the Spring Festival has come, and the peasants have been taught to be ever grateful to, and appreciative of, the goodness of their Father, for all the benefits they have received, and for another springtime; believing that, upon the quantity of boughs and leaves with which they decorate their homes, will depend the fruitfulness of the coming crops. And thus, with great joy, is spring welcomed in Poland.

CHAPTER VIII

THE ORPHANAGE IN THE WOODS

AS the spring season advanced, the two children at the dwór grew more and more excited. They were awaiting, with great impatience, the arrival of St. John's Eve, the 24th of June.

Marya was seated upon the stiff-looking sofa in the reception salon, while her brother Peter was looking through a book of photographs, depicting the celebration of the Wianki.

"Do you suppose mother will allow us to cast a wreath into the Vistula?" asked Peter, without looking up from his book, so intensely wrapped up was he in the illustrations.

"Certainly," Marya replied. "If we go to the celebration at all, we will be allowed to do as the others do. I shall ask her," Marya continued, "for it wouldn't be a bit of fun to go all the way to Cracow just to watch the others; I want some of the fun for myself."

"You don't imagine you will be allowed to go in search of the wonderful fern, do you, Marya?" the boy questioned.

"Why not? Of course I know I may not go alone, but I shall have Mademoiselle with me. It would be quite proper then, and Mademoiselle would enjoy it herself, I am sure. She has never seen the celebration, Peter, and she's just as crazy over it as we are. If sister Martha comes we will be allowed to go," the girl continued, "for she knows what it is to be shut off from every pleasure that even the commonest people have."

"Marya," warned Peter, in a low tone.

At the warning, the girl looked up. She saw her mother upon the threshold. She arose instantly from her seat upon the sofa and advanced toward her mother, saluting her with a kiss upon the cheek. Her brother did likewise, and together they gently led her toward the sofa and seated her, drawing up two chairs for themselves, so as to face her. But Marya did not seat herself by the side of her mother. It is a curious custom throughout Europe that the sofa is the seat of honor, to be occupied by the person highest in rank, and, while one may occupy a sofa when alone in the room, it is considered the height of impoliteness to seat one's self upon that sacred article of furniture when one of superior rank, or an elder, is in the room; therefore it was for this reason that the children placed their mother upon the sofa while they occupied chairs by her side.

"Now, children, listen," Mrs. Ostrowska said, as she gathered her two children to her. "You need not be a bit afraid that you will not enjoy yourselves in Cracow. I have promised to take you to the celebration of the Wianki, and you have looked forward to it for a long time with great expectation. You shall not be disappointed. We will forget everything for that night, and you may enter into all the sports of the people, if you choose. Even Marya, dear, if she wishes, may penetrate into the depths of the forest and search for the sacred fern which may blossom for her alone this year. Perhaps you may be the fortunate one to find it, Marya. What do you think?"

"I hope I shall," the girl replied. "But suppose Mademoiselle should become frightened and want to return?"

"In that event," the mother said, smiling, "so long as you have the courage, you may continue alone," for she felt quite safe in granting this privilege, as she did not truly believe her little daughter would be brave enough to continue alone.

"When shall we start?" Marya asked, in great excitement.

"It is now the twentieth of June," Mrs. Ostrowska replied. "Your father has some business to attend to in Cracow, so we shall leave here on the twenty-second, which will give us ample time to look about the city and have a good visit with your sister Martha, for you know she promised to meet us there."

"So did sister Gabriele," added Peter.

"Yes," the mother replied, "we shall all be together, I hope."

"And may I go now and tell Mademoiselle?" Marya inquired, eagerly, as she rose.

"Run along," the mother answered. "And what was my boy reading as I came in?" she continued, turning to her son, who had not had a chance to say much while the irrepressible sister was in the room.

"Oh, I was looking at some old books I found in the library, about the celebration of the Wianki. I wanted to know all about it; there are some wonderful pictures of it too."

"It is a curious custom, no doubt," the mother replied, as she walked to the table, where the book still remained open. And, for some time, the two looked over the great volume of illustrations, remarking every little while about this one or that.

"You remember the story of the Princess Wanda, and how she threw herself into the Vistula in order to save her country from wars?" the mother asked.

"Very well, indeed," the boy replied. "She was a brave princess. But is it really true, mother?" the boy inquired.

"There was a Princess Wanda at one time, but as to the rest of the story, that is what people say about her."

At this moment Marya re-entered the room, leading her governess by the hand.

"Mother," the child said, as she advanced toward the table where the mother and son were engrossed in their book, "Mademoiselle is as delighted as I am, with the prospect of seeing the celebration, aren't you, Mademoiselle?"

"Indeed I am," the young lady replied. "I have read much about it, in France, but have never witnessed one of the festivals; besides, it happens to be my birthday, so it will be an added pleasure."

"I have arranged for the children of the Orphanage to come out to us just after our return," Mrs. Ostrowska said, addressing the tall, bright-eyed young lady who served in capacity of governess to her daughter; "I wish you would take Marya down to the Bosquet and help prepare the cottage for their reception. The maids are there now, airing the place out, and I will drive over later in the afternoon, when I shall have everything together that I want sent down."

"Very well, Madame," Mademoiselle replied. "Marya and I will attend to it as soon as luncheon is finished. Shall we take the pony cart?"

"Yes, you might," Mrs. Ostrowska said, "and, when you arrive there, see that the beds are well aired, for the maids are apt to be a little careless, and we can't afford to have any of the children take cold."

"There's luncheon now," Marya called out, impulsively.

"Run along then, children," the mistress said, "and remember, day after to-morrow we are off for Cracow."

With hurried steps the two children left the room, followed by Mademoiselle, while Mrs. Ostrowska busied herself about her domestic arrangements, for she never entrusted these duties to any one.

After luncheon Marya and Mademoiselle drove off in the pony cart, through the beautiful gardens, which were blossoming with all sorts of magnificent flowers, past the great fish-ponds at the rear, and on through the thick woods. Finally they pulled rein at a most picturesque maisonette, or cottage, situated in the very heart of the forest. It was built of logs; a wide veranda ran across the entire front. The house was large enough to accommodate one hundred girls with their chaperones. Inside everything was as comfortable as could be. There was a general sitting-room where the orphaned girls could gather in the evening and listen to the folk-tales their hostess or her substitutes would tell. There were great dormitories, with twenty or thirty snowy, white beds arranged in rows against the walls, with large airy windows between. There was the dining-room, with its long table spread with good, substantial food; and how the walls did ring with the laughter and joyousness of these little orphaned children from the city, who were invited each year to spend two weeks or more as the guests of the benevolent proprietor's wife, Mrs. Ostrowska. And all over the country of Poland this is the custom for the wives of the landed proprietors to do. They give of their wealth for the betterment of the poor and to ease their burden a little.

Each morning a group of girls, selected by the mistress in charge, tramp off through the woods, baskets on arms, to receive from the kitchen of the dwór the supplies for the following day; and you may be sure this is no small matter, to fill fifty or one hundred hungry mouths. In the afternoons, after the day's work is finished, for these girls do all their own housekeeping in the maisonette, they gather berries or wood-flowers, which they present to their kind hostess, a delicate thoughtfulness which she fully appreciates, for these poor little orphaned ones have no other way in which to express their gratitude for the pleasures they accept.

Everything being in readiness, Marya and her governess returned home through the woods, driving leisurely so as to enjoy the fresh odor of the firs. It was quite late when they reached the dwór; tea was being served on the veranda. Here they sought out Mrs. Ostrowska and reported their progress. Then Marya was whisked off by Mademoiselle to attend to her practising.

The morning of the twenty-second dawned bright and warm. Immediately after breakfast, the great carriage pulled up at the porch, and all were soon installed within. The whips were cracked, and away the horses sped down the wide avenue of linden trees, through the great stone brama and out into the country road. They had not gone very far when the animals were reined in most emphatically, for the highway had become a horrible mass of mud and ruts. The public roads of Poland are proverbial for their wretchedness. The carriage swayed from side to side as it lurched from one deep rut into another; and had it not been for the splendid springs of the carriage, it would have been much more comfortable to have walked. You may imagine what it would mean to jolt over these same roads in a britschka, or public cart, which is so widely in use in Poland. It is a sort of open carriage, without springs of any kind, with a hood which can either be raised or lowered, at the will of the occupant. I fear a ride in such a contrivance would not be very enjoyable. However, in spite of the ill condition of the road, Cracow was reached safely late in the afternoon. Upon reaching the hotel where accommodations had been reserved, they found the two sisters awaiting them.

Mrs. Ostrowska had found the journey very fatiguing, consequently she did not care to dress and descend for dinner; dinner, therefore, was served upstairs in her private sitting-room, and the family spent the remainder of the evening in discussing their plans for the morrow, and in visiting.

CHAPTER IX

WHAT HAPPENED WHEN THE BROTHERS DISAGREED

IT is market-day in Cracow; but then it is always market-day in Cracow, so that would be nothing extraordinary. The rynek, or square, is crowded with groups of peasants, some sitting on stools beside their vegetables exposed for sale; others sheltered under huge umbrellas, knitting stockings for their family, while awaiting customers. Here are displayed laces, vegetables, also chickens and ducks, alive and squawking. There is scarcely anything one would have need of that is not displayed in this square. Indeed, it is a lively spot and a beautiful sight.

We have some hours to pass before evening comes, when we may ascend to the Wawel for the celebration; therefore, we shall look about us in this active part of the city and see some of the interesting sights and ancient buildings, for most cities are interesting only as they can present some historical reference. Here is an ancient-looking castle at this side of the rynek; indeed, it not only looks ancient, but it is ancient. Like everything else in Poland, it has a queer-sounding name to us; it is known as Pod Baranami, which means Under the Ram's Head, from its heraldic sign over the front. This is the home of the Potockis, one of the very ancient families of the country. So prominent is this castle in the history of Poland that the Emperor has chosen it as his residence when he is in the city of Cracow. But it would be quite improper for the Emperor to accept quarters in the home of another; he must be the veritable head of the house; therefore it happens that, from an old custom, it is usual for the family to move to other quarters and to permit the sovereign full possession. The Emperor, however, is not without graciousness. He accepts the generosity of his subject, and atones for the inconvenience he has been put to by inviting the owner and his family to dine with him. It must seem very strange to be invited to dinner in one's own home with another at the head.

And here, a little further along, is the most interesting building known as the Sukiennice, nothing more nor less than the Cloth Hall. In early days, when there were no great department stores and selling agents for goods, the makers of cloth formed a guild or club, which became known throughout the land as the Cloth Guild. They built a great hall in which to display their goods, for there were no shops in those times, as there are now. This building became known as the Cloth Hall. Here the Guild met to discuss the prices they should askfor the finished material, and how much they ought to pay for the raw. The Cloth Guild was one of the richest and most influential of all the Guilds, for people were extravagant in their dress and wore most exquisite materials.

The Sukiennice is a great building of stone with the stairway to the second story running up on the outside of the building; there are queer little turrets, one at each corner, and heavy arcades upon the ground floor, which protect the passers-by from the elements, as well as assist in rendering the interior very dark.

Here, in the city of Cracow, the peasants will tell you of a curious belief among them. The founder of Poland was Lekh, as you all have read. He was supposed to have come from the far south, when quite a grown man; but there are always two sides to every story, as the saying is. And no two historians can agree as to which version is really the correct one concerning Lekh. The peasants here believe that Lekh was born in this very city, and they absolutely refuse to believe anything else. In any event, the story goes that when he was a very young baby, as he was lying in his cradle one day, without any one near, a fierce dragon with three heads tried to devour him; but no harm came to the child, for he grew up safely to manhood. Perhaps his faithful nurse returned in time to avert the threatened danger. However, many, many years later, in this same city of Cracow, in the year 1846, the country of Poland suffered its greatest humiliation, for Cracow was the very last city in the country to fall into the hands of the enemy. And now once more comes the dragon with the three heads; it is the enemy, Austria, Germany and Russia, who joined their forces together to tear beloved Poland into pieces, and this time it won the victory.

The people of Poland will tell you that once upon a time, in the early days of the country's history, there was a certain king reigning over the land, who was very good and wise. He saw that his beloved people and the land in which they lived was not what it should be; that something was wrong.

Being a solicitous father for his country, he left no stone unturned to discover some remedy for the malady which ailed Poland. Physicians, famed throughout the land, were sent for and consultations held, but all in vain. There seemed no cure for the patient. However, there was yet one resource left. In the land was a woman who was very clever at divinations; to her, in his last extremity, the good, kind king went and stated his trouble.

"Fear not," the prophetess answered, after listening to the king's tale, "I will endeavor to aid you."

The king was delighted at her encouraging words, but he felt somewhat doubtful of the result, as so many had failed before her. The old woman selected three brothers from out the land; to each of them she gave a third part of a flute.

"You are to journey together," she said to them, "until you have crossed over seven mountains, and crossed seven flowing rivers. When you reach a certain peak in the Carpathian Mountains to the southwest of Poland, you are to halt, put the pieces of the flute together, and blow upon it. At the sound, your brave old king, Boleslaw, and his valiant knights, will arise from their sleep of death, take up their weapons, and conquer your enemy, when Poland will once more be restored to her former state of splendor and glory."

The king thanked the prophetess kindly, adding a most substantial gift for her services. He saw the three brothers set off upon their task of salvation for the country.

The three young men journeyed together, as they had been bid, until they crossed seven running rivers and had climbed over seven mountains. At length they reached the Carpathian Mountains as the old woman had told them. Upon the top of the peak she had named they halted, and pieced the flute together. Then arose the important question of which they had not thought before: who should blow upon the flute.

The oldest brother thought he should, for was he not the eldest? The second brother thought he had just as much right to blow upon the flute as his older brother. Why should he have all the glory when they, too, had made the long journey as well as the eldest? But the youngest brother was not content with this arrangement. He felt that he should have a turn at the flute as well as the other two. And, in this manner, they bickered and bickered. The days sped by without the question being settled. And thus it remained. As they could not agree as to which one should blow upon the flute, no one blew upon it. King Boleslaw did not awaken from his sleep. His knights, in their suits of armor, remained by his side, tranquil and at rest, and Poland, poor Poland, the ill one, was left to its fate. The legend runs, that the names of the three brothers were Aristocracy, Bourgeoisie and Peasantry. And to-day, were they given another opportunity to show their worth, there would be no question as to which one of the three would blow upon the flute, for all Poland has agreed that its hope and life are due to the youngest brother, Peasantry. And in this hope the upper class Polacks are bending every effort towards improving the condition and education of the common people, for thereby they believe the day will come when the peasantry will arise, like the knights of King Boleslaw, and fight for their liberty. The inference is that the peasants are now asleep; they do not see theiropportunities, nor know their strength; but that when they do arise they will bring peace and prosperity once more to dear Poland.

Peter and Marya were so interested in the history of the city, and in looking at its magnificent old buildings, they were not aware how rapidly the time was passing, until their mother told them it was time to return to the hotel for dinner. As soon as the first rays of dusk crept on, they insisted upon making their way to the Wawel, so as not to miss anything; for well they knew, these little children of the aristocracy, they would not be again permitted this privilege. As they drove from the hotel to the top of the hill they passed great crowds, and yet more and more, all making their way on foot up the toilsome incline to the castle, the one spot of activity that night.

A bright fire was already burning within the fortress courtyard. The flames leaped higher and higher until they fairly seemed to reach to the vaulted blue above. About the fire were gathered thousands and thousands of people: old men and women, young men and their wives and sweethearts, for the entire populace had turned out to celebrate the Wianki, or wreaths. Each one bore in his hand a wreath of flowers or leaves, all of different colors; and while the band played entrancing music, wild polonaises and mazurkas, the people cast their wreaths into the waters of the Vistula. Brilliant fireworks of every description lighted up the scene, making the sky one mass of light and color. Every one looked very happy and gave himself up to the joy of the moment.

The wreaths having been cast into the river, the young folks joined hands in a great circle about the blazing fire. They danced round and round, singing Polish airs; strangers all they were, but enjoying each other's company. From among the circle, two young folks were chosen, a man and a young girl, the circle of singers coupling the names of the two together, prophesying that these two might become affianced and wed happily. What mattered it that they were unknown to each other? What mattered anything that night, when all hearts were light, and youth was abroad?

In games and sports of this character, the evening wore away and the hour of midnight approached. Marya was becoming more and more excited. She grasped the hand of Mademoiselle tighter, for fear she should lose her; then she might not penetrate into the forest.

One by one the young girls of the group slipped away and disappeared into the gloom of the surrounding woods; Marya believed it was about time that she, too, were making good her escape. Holding tightly to the hand of her governess, she walked slowly in the direction the others had taken. She had at last set out on her search for the magic fern which grows in the forest. She would try to discover its hiding-place; for she longed for a happy and successful life. It is no small task, this, that Marya had set for herself. In the first place the fern is magic; it is not to be seen by every one; it blooms just a second, exactly as the midnight hour strikes, and then is gone. And another full year must roll by before the maiden may search a second time.

"HER HEART WAS BEATING FASTER AND FASTER"

"I shall find it," Marya kept repeating to herself, over and over again. But she knew she could not hope to do so if she persisted in holding fast to the hand of Mademoiselle. No one must have an escort who would find the precious flower. But Marya was timid. Never before had she been permitted out after dark, even alone with her governess. The woods were very dark. The moon shone through the leaves, 'tis true, but the beams only added to the fright of the young girl, for they cast weird shadows upon the tree-trunks and more than once she was for turning back.

She dared not call out for fear of breaking the magic spell, and she did so want to find the magic fern.

Her heart was beating faster and faster; she groped her way through the thick trees, keeping her eyes riveted upon the ground in search of the prize. Suddenly she saw a bright light ahead of her. She wondered what it could be; whether it was some sprite's home in the forest, and what was going to happen to her next. Then she heard the tinkle of a bell. "The hejnal," she told herself. "Midnight." She counted the strokes one by one. So intent was she upon her task that she forgot the magic fern. She forgot Mademoiselle. She forgot everything but the musical tones of the church bell tolling the midnight hour. She kept her course toward the light in the distance. When she approached it, she found herself once more on the Wawel hill, by the side of the great fire about which she had danced so happily the early part of the evening. She had been walking in a circle; and there, not ten feet from her, was Mademoiselle; but neither of them had discovered the magic fern.

"Well, it was fun anyway," Marya said, when twitted by her brother for her failure. "And I am sure if I could try again, I would walk in a straight line next time."

The party returned to the hotel; the festival was ended, and on the morrow the Ostrowski family returned to their dwór beyond Cracow.

CHAPTER X

THE HARVEST FESTIVAL

AND now our vacation is about ended. The year is drawing to a close. Harvest time has arrived; the crops are stacked up in the fields to be garnered in.

The peasants have finished their year's work out-of-doors. They have served their master's interests well; all that remains is his inspection to see that all is satisfactory, and his approval that they earned their wages.

Mr. Ostrowski, accompanied by his good wife, left their home upon the hill and walked towards the great fields of yellow grain. It was not permitted the peasant to garner in these sheaves until the master had passed by. Suddenly, they were seized from behind. Theywere seized gently but forcibly. While one young man held the wrists of the mistress, and others the wrists of the master, other peasants picked up strands of the golden straw and assisted in securely binding their captives. The master and mistress pleaded for their liberty, but their captors were adamant. No ransom, no liberty. At length, after promises of ransom, the peasants unbound their victims, the money was paid over, and the master and mistress were free. Laughing, they passed on their way across the field, while the merry peasants then began to stack the golden grain upon their carts and haul it away to the barns.

It is a very pretty custom, this one of the Harvest Festival; and master and laborer enter into the spirit of it with keen zest. It but endears their patron to them the more that he permits this privilege; the ransom is not more than a few pennies; but the master must pay it before he may regain his liberty. All over the estate, from one field to the other, the same ceremony is indulged in for the harvest crops.

What merry-making there is in the village during the rest of the day and all through the evening, after the crops are safely stowed away for the winter!

The fairest maiden of the village is the queen of the day. She wears her white dress with a queenly air, too; and holds her proud head high, crowned with flowers. Forming in line, the queen at the head, the bridesmaids following, and then the other villagers in the order of their importance, the gay procession marches slowly up the hill, singing folk songs as they mount. Their sweet, musical voices announce their arrival long beforehand to the mistress of the dwór. She meets them at the porch with graciousness. The queen kneels for her mistress' blessing, and once more they return down the hill toward the village, but now they are enriched with a quantity of small money, with which they straightway proceed to set up a supper, after which they dance the rest of the hours away. They have good cause to be light-hearted, for they know their work is finished for the season, and there are full barns for the winter.

And we have now spent a full year in the delightful, quaint land of Lekh; dear Poland, from whose brow has never vanished the one cloud that mars it. It has learned its tragic lesson too late, that what it does not sow it may not reap. The nobles had been too much enwrapped in their own gayety, in their exclusiveness, to turn their hands to the task of setting things straight. The bourgeoisie were neither of one class nor another; they could not afford to compromise themselves by turning either way, consequently they turned neither, and were useless as aids. The peasants were raised in ignorance, were overburdened and kept constantly under the leash, so to speak, and while their strength might have saved the country, they had not the brain-power to solve a means therefor. So that neither of the three brothers being able to decide which should blow upon the flute, as neither class would take upon itself to save the land, so they now await the decision. In the meantime, Poland belongs to the three conquering nations, the Russians, the Austrians and the Germans, neither of which the Polacks are devoted to.

And yet, with all its indecision, Poland has given the world some glorious men and women. Copernicus, the world-famed astrologer, was born in the city of Thorn upon the River Vistula, on February 19, 1473. Chopin, the great musical composer, was the son of a Polish woman, although he is buried in France. Marcella Sembrich, Edouard De Reszke and his brother Jean, of grand opera fame, Helena Modjeska, our beloved actress, now passed away, and Jan Paderewski, the celebrated pianist, are all Polacks.

And we Americans have much to be indebted for to a great Polish soldier. You may not even know his name; had it not been for Tadeusz Kosciuszko, I doubt very much whether Washington, our dearly beloved George Washington, would have proven so successful in his endeavors for independence.

It is a long way from Warsaw in Poland to the American colonies; especially was it so in the year 1776, when transportation was not what it now is. But Tadeusz did not consider distance or hardship. He was willing to go anywhere, so long as it would take him from the place where he had suffered so keenly. For back in Poland, Tadeusz loved a beautiful girl. The father of this young lady did not approve of Kosciuszko as a lover. He feared the two might elope, which they had really planned to do. Therefore, he carried off his daughter inthe dead of night, so that Tadeusz never saw her again.

Kosciuszko roamed first here and then there in his sorrow; he did not care much where he went to. At last he went to Paris. All the modern world was talking about the courage of the American colonists in taking up their struggle against the mother country. And it happened that during his stay in Paris, Kosciuszko chanced to meet our minister, Benjamin Franklin. When Franklin learned that Tadeusz was skilled in military tactics, and, furthermore, that it made no particular difference to him where he strayed, he at once offered to give him a letter to Washington. Our general was indeed glad to receive such a valuable aid, and appointed him colonel of engineers and placed him upon his staff. Soon his proficiency in fort-building won for him the honor of scientist of the American Army. He worked by the side of Washington for eight years, until he was no longer needed. Then he returned to Poland, for his heart was ever there. He gained a glorious victory, the victory of Raclawie, which the Polacks can never forget. They have erected a mound to his honor, and even the American government has not been ungrateful to this grand man.

Another Polack, Count Casimir Pulaski, also served us well in our early struggles; he was killed at the battle of Savannah in 1779.

Henryk Sienkiewicz has given us some wonderful masterpieces in literature, and there are countless other Polish authors who might be mentioned, but they are too numerous and one is not as familiar with their works as with those of Sienkiewicz.

We may linger no longer. The Christmas season approaches, when we must return to our own again. Homewards we turn our steps, with intense regret. We leave behind us the flat, broad plains of Lekh, we recross the Continent, take ship at Havre, and are once again in our beloved America, where we see our poor happy and comfortable; where all is bustle and prosperity, and we feel thankful that our independence has lasted throughout these years and that no nation may come in and rob us of our heritage.

THE END.